The Case
of the
Chewable
Worms

Tommy Nelson® Books by Bill Myers

Series

SECRET AGENT DINGLEDORF
. . . and his trusty dog, SPLAT 🐾

The Case of the Giggling Geeks
The Case of the Chewable Worms
The Case of the Flying Toenails

The Incredible Worlds of
Wally McDoogle

—*My Life As a Smashed Burrito with Extra Hot Sauce*
—*My Life As Alien Monster Bait*
—*My Life As a Broken Bungee Cord*
—*My Life As Crocodile Junk Food*
—*My Life As Dinosaur Dental Floss*
—*My Life As a Torpedo Test Target*
—*My Life As a Human Hockey Puck*
—*My Life As an Afterthought Astronaut*
—*My Life As Reindeer Road Kill*
—*My Life As a Toasted Time Traveler*
—*My Life As Polluted Pond Scum*
—*My Life As a Bigfoot Breath Mint*
—*My Life As a Blundering Ballerina*
—*My Life As a Screaming Skydiver*
—*My Life As a Human Hairball*
—*My Life As a Walrus Whoopee Cushion*
—*My Life As a Computer Cockroach (Mixed-Up Millennium Bug)*
—*My Life As a Beat-Up Basketball Backboard*
—*My Life As a Cowboy Cowpie*
—*My Life As Invisible Intestines with Intense Indigestion*
—*My Life As a Skysurfing Skateboarder*

Picture Book
Baseball for Breakfast

www.Billmyers.com

SECRET AGENT
DINGLEDORF
. . . and his trusty dog, SPLAT

The Case of the Chewable Worms

BILL MYERS

Illustrations
Meredith Johnson

Tommy
NELSON

www.tommynelson.com

A Division of Thomas Nelson, Inc.
www.ThomasNelson.com

THE CASE OF THE CHEWABLE WORMS

Text copyright © 2002 by Bill Myers
Illustrations by Meredith Johnson. Copyright © 2002 by Tommy Nelson®, a Division of Thomas Nelson, Inc., Nashville, Tennessee.

Published in Nashville, Tennessee, by Tommy Nelson®, a Division of Thomas Nelson, Inc.

Scripture quotations noted ICB are from the *International Children's Bible*®, *New Century Version*® © 1986, 1989, 1999 by Tommy Nelson®, a Division of Thomas Nelson, Inc., Nashville, Tennessee 37214. Used by permission.

Library of Congress Cataloging-in-Publication Data

Myers, Bill, 1953–
    The case of the chewable worms / by Bill Myers.
        p. cm.
    ISBN: 1-4003-0095-9
    [1. Spies—Fiction. 2. Christian life—Fiction. 3. Humorous stories.]
I. Title.
pz7.M98234 Caq 2002
[Fic]—dc21   2002070934

Printed in the United States of America

05 06 RRD 8

For Mrs. Schuyler
and her second-grade class.
Thanks for the help!

"We must not become tired of doing good. . . . We must not give up! When we have the opportunity to help anyone, we should do it."

—Galatians 6:9–10 (ICB)

Contents

CHAPTER 1

The Case Begins . . .

"**W**here is everybody?" I.Q. asked.

He sniffed and pushed up his glasses. I.Q. always sniffs and pushes up his glasses. The poor guy is allergic to everything . . . especially being cool.

I looked around the playground. He was right. It was emptier than our refrigerator after my sister's boyfriend visits.

"What's going on?" Priscilla, another friend, asked. Even though she's a girl, we let her hang around. (If we didn't, she'd beat us up. She's pretty good at karate, karaoke, and all that self-defense stuff.) "Where is everyone?" she asked.

"Wait a minute." I pointed to the far end of the playground. "Everybody's over there!"

Off in the distance we saw about a million kids. They were kneeling down in the dirt and yelling.

"What are they up to?" Priscilla asked.

"Perhaps we should *(sniff)* join them and *(sniff, sniff)* find out," I.Q. said.

"Great idea," I said. (That's why we keep I.Q. around. He always has great ideas.)

"Maybe they're playing marbles," I said.

"Or maybe jacks," Priscilla offered.

"Or maybe calculating the formula to Einstein's theory of relativity!" I.Q. said. (Okay, so sometimes his ideas aren't so great.)

As we got closer, we saw that they were racing.

But they weren't racing each other.

Instead, they were down in the mud, racing . . .

"Worms?!" Priscilla shouted. "They're racing worms?!"

She was right. If there were a million kids there, then there were a hundred million worms. Mounds of them . . .

slithering,
        slinking,
               and squirming . . .

all over each other. And all over the kids!

"What's happening?" I shouted as we arrived. But no one answered. They were all too busy yelling and screaming:

"Let's go, Gooey!"

"Come on, Slimy!"

"You can do it, Slick!"

"Where did you obtain all of these *(sniff)* worms?" I.Q. shouted.

"From home!" a sixth grader yelled back.

"Our moms packed them in our lunch boxes," a second grader explained.

Then, just when things couldn't get any weirder:

beep-beep-beep-beep

I.Q. and Priscilla turned to me.

Even over the shouting they could hear it. But I pretended not to notice.

beep-beep-beep-beep

"Bernie?" Priscilla yelled.

I looked at her. "What?"

"Your underwear. It's . . .

ringing again."

"I know!" I shouted. "It's been doing that all morning."

"Aren't you going to answer it?" she asked.

"If I do, I'll have to solve another case and save the world!" I said.

"But you're a secret agent. That's what secret agents do!"

She was only half right. That *is* what secret agents do. But I really wasn't a secret agent. The government got me mixed up with somebody else. Of course, I keep trying to tell them that, but they won't listen. (The fact that I keep solving cases doesn't help.)

I hoped that by ignoring their calls to my secret agent underpants . . .

they'd leave me alone.

"Come on, Bernie," I.Q. said. "Don't you want to help people?"

"I'm always helping people," I complained.

"But helping them is good," he said.

I shrugged. "Maybe. Or maybe if people get themselves into trouble they should be the ones to get themselves out."

I knew that sounded kinda selfish. But I also knew that's how I was feeling.

Little did I realize how soon those feelings would change. . . .

Later in the afternoon we sat in a school assembly watching

WENDY WING-NUT'S WONDERFUL WORLD OF WORMS

It was like a circus act. But instead of lions and tigers, or even dogs, she had (you guessed it) . . . worms.

Worms climbing up ladders.

Worms jumping through flaming hoops.

Worms with Wendy sticking her head in their mouths.

(Well, okay, not really—but everything else was true.)

Then, for a little comedy, she did magic tricks. The best was when she pretended to pull a worm out of Mrs. Hooplesnort's

ear. Later, she had them crawling out of Principal Lecture's hair.

Of course, we all laughed. But even then I suspected something wasn't exactly right.

At the end of the assembly, Mrs. Wing-Nut asked, "And do you know the best part about these worms, boys and girls?"

"What?" we shouted back.

"They're chewable!"

Suddenly, she popped a handful into her mouth and began chewing!

"Yum!" she said, careful to swallow before grinning.

But instead of the normal

"Ick!"

"Gross!" or

"I think I'm going to be sick,"

the kids started to cheer.

Some even reached into their own pockets, pulled out their own worms, and began chomping away!

Mrs. Wing-Nut's grin grew bigger. "Well, I can see your mommies and daddies have already been serving them to you."

"You bet!" they shouted.

"Aren't they yummy?"

"You bet!" they shouted some more.

"And for those of you who haven't tried them, what are you waiting for?! We're giving away free samples at the door!"

"Yea!" the kids shouted.

"And tell your friends," Mrs. Wing-Nut shouted. "The more, the merrier."

At last the assembly ended and we headed for the doors.

I turned to Priscilla and I.Q. "This is too weird," I said.

"Slimy worms." Priscilla shuddered. "Why is everybody so crazy about them?"

"Perhaps (*sniff*) it's a UFO invasion," I.Q. said.

"You think everything is a UFO invasion," I said.

He shrugged. "It never hurts to be (*sniff, sniff*) prepared."

"Look!" Priscilla pointed to a first grader. A bunch of his friends were telling him to take one of the sample worms and eat it.

You could tell he didn't want to do it. But his friends kept on bugging him.

Finally, he put one into his mouth.

"All right!" they cheered.

Then, the weirdest thing of all happened: The kid's eyes lit up and he started grabbing more worms.

The other kids clapped and offered some of their own. Soon his pockets (not to mention his mouth) were overflowing with the squishy squirmers.

"Something's definitely bad in a not-so-good way," I said.

"Shouldn't we warn them?" I.Q. asked.

I shook my head. "It's really none of our business."

"Yeah, but . . ."

"If they want to be gross, let them be gross. As long as it doesn't hurt us, who cares?"

Little did I realize how wrong I'd be.

CHAPTER 2

Soup's On

Eating dinner at our house is like going to the movies. But instead of watching one movie, you get to watch three . . . all at the same time.

Let me introduce you to our stars.

First, there is Sister 1, better known as . . .

THE PROM QUEEN
"If Jeremy doesn't ask me out, I'll just die. I mean, he's like the cutest boy in the whole senior class and . . ."

Then there's Sister 2 . . .

THE GOSSIP QUEEN

"Did you see Bonnie holding Buddy's hand when she thought Bradley wasn't watching Beverly watching Billy who . . ."

And last, but not least, Sister 3 . . .

THE FASHION QUEEN

"This beaded dress is so incredibly retro. I'll have to lose a couple of pounds to wear it, but . . ."

Mix them all together and you have something that sounds like:

"This beaded dress isn't talking to you but I'll just about Bradley's like . . .

That's why I ignored them and focused on more important things. Like eating.

At least that's what I tried to focus on. But tonight was a little different.

"Mom?"

"Yes, sweetheart?"

"How come the noodles in my soup are squirming?"

"Oh, they're not squirming, sweetheart, they're swimming."

"Oh." I frowned. "Uh, Mom?"

"Yes, dear?"

"How come the noodles in my soup are swimming?"

"Oh, they're not noodles, dear."

"They're not?"

"Of course not, silly." She scooped up a giant spoonful and slurped them into her mouth. "Mhey're mworms!" (It should have been "They're worms!" but her mouth was stuffed with the critters.)

"Worms?!" I cried.

"Yes." She grinned. "Aren't they yummy?"

I stared at my soup in horror.

She turned to Dad. "And what do you think, Walter?"

"Delicious," he grunted. (Dad always grunts. With three daughters yakking away all the time, that's the only sound he can squeeze in.)

"This is great, Mom," Prom Queen said as she slurped. "Where did you get them?"

"The store was giving free samples!"

Gossip Queen giggled with delight. "Wait 'til I tell Brian not to tell Burt not to tell . . . " (She would have kept going, but she was too busy shoveling the wigglers into her mouth.)

Then there was Fashion Queen. "I suppose one won't make me too fat. Or two or three . . . or thirteen or twenty . . . "

"Mom!" I cried.

"Just try one bite, dear," she said. "After that, you'll love them, too."

I looked around the table. I didn't believe it. Everyone just kept on

sipping and *slurping*

away.

Finally, Mom rose from the table. "And wait until you see our main course," she said as she headed into the kitchen.

I was afraid to guess. Unfortunately, I didn't have to.

A moment later she returned, carrying a giant platter of spaghetti and meatballs.

But, as you probably figured, the spaghetti wasn't exactly spaghetti. (You could tell by the way the noodles slithered over the meatballs.)

Luckily, it was about this time that my underpants started

beep-beep-beep-beep-ing.

Even luckier, everybody was too busy eating to hear.

I quickly excused myself and ran for the stairs.

Unfortunately, these are the same stairs that Splat the Wonder-dog sleeps at the top of.

No problem, except for the part of tripping over him, causing him to leap up in the middle of his sleep, and

"Woof! Woof!"

slip off the top step and

K-thud
K-thud
K-thud

all the way down the stairs until he finally

K-Splat-ed

into the opposite wall. (Well, at least now you know how he got his name.)

"Splat? Are you okay?" I shouted.

He gave a little whine for sympathy. (Splat always goes for the sympathy.)

Then he zoomed back up the stairs to join me. (Actually, with his chubby body it was more crawling than zooming. But at last he made it.)

Good ol' Splat.

By the time we got to my room, my underpants had quit ringing.

But the mirror on my dresser had begun talking!

"Hello, Secret Agent Dingledorf."

I spun around. Sure enough, it was the head of the agency, Big Guy. Well, at least his reflection.

"How did you get in there?" I asked.

"Just another one of our secret agent gizmos," he said. "Why haven't you been answering my calls?"

"I've told you a hundred times, I'm not a secret agent!"

"People need your help."

"I'm not interested."

"That's what you've been saying."

"Look," I said, "I've got my own problems, okay?"

"Maybe by helping others, you'd be helping solve your problems."

"Not unless their problems involve—"

"Worms?" he asked.

I looked at him in surprise. Suddenly, his reflection was replaced by a football game. But instead of the usual bashing and bruising, the teams were on their hands and knees slurping up, you guessed it . . .

Worms!

The fans weren't doing any better. They were cheering away. But instead of chowing down on hot buttered popcorn, they were chowing down on hot buttered worms!

"That's gross!" I cried.

"It gets worse," Big Guy answered. "Look at this."

Suddenly, the image in the mirror changed to a news conference.

It was the president. But instead of reporters asking him important questions, they were asking:

"Mr. President? Do you like your worms baked or boiled?"

"Is there any truth to the rumor that you prefer them barbecued?"

"What's going on?" I cried.

Big Guy came back in the mirror. "It's B.A.D.D.," he said.

"Yes, it's terrible."

"No," he said, "I mean it's the organization B.A.D.D."

"Who?"

"**B**ungling **A**gents **D**edicated to **D**estruction."

"Destruction of what?" I asked.

"The destruction of us," he said.

"I don't understand."

He explained. "B.A.D.D. has invented a worm that is so tasty it's habit-forming. Once you eat one, you can't stop. Soon, the entire world will fall under their power. Soon, all anyone will want to do is eat worms."

"What's that got to do with me?" I asked. "As long as I don't eat any, I'll be okay."

"What about your friends and family?"

I shrugged. "I guess they'll have to look out for themselves."

"But they need your help!"

"Sorry," I said. "I've got enough to worry about with just me."

"But—"

"Look, I've got to get ready for bed."

"But—"

"Sorry, Big Guy. You'll just have to find somebody else."

With that, his image disappeared.

Good, I thought. I went to the bathroom to brush my teeth.

I felt kind of bad for Big Guy (not to mention the rest of the world). But a fellow has to look out for himself, right?

I grabbed the toothpaste, squeezed it onto my brush, and let out a gasp. Because it wasn't toothpaste. Now it was, you guessed it . . .

WORMS!

CHAPTER 3

"I'm Out of Here!"

Do you have a sister? If you do, you know how hard it is to use the bathroom in the morning.

And with three sisters, it's three times as hard.

On good days they give me seven seconds to shower.

On bad days, like the next morning, I got zero.

The reason was simple. Once they showered they had to put on their worm lipstick, their worm lip gloss, and, of course, use their new worm mouthwash.

Breakfast wasn't much better. Mom

was making bacon and eggs. But the bacon looked a lot skinnier than I remembered . . . and a lot more wiggly.

I passed on breakfast.

I headed back to my room and put on some of my secret agent clothes. I also grabbed my secret agent backpack . . . just in case. Things were getting crazy. It wouldn't hurt to be prepared.

The backpack felt heavier than I remembered. But I didn't have time to check inside. Mom was coming toward me with something in her hands.

"Here, dear," she said. "Don't forget to take these nice new pencils."

"Mom," I said, "look at the way they're twisting and squirming. Those aren't pencils!"

"They're worm pencils," she explained. "Not only do they write, but when you're done, they make tasty snacks!"

"No, thanks," I said as I raced past her and out the door.

"Are you sure?" she called after me. She tossed a "pencil" into her mouth. "Don't you want to try just . . .

chomp, chomp
gulp, gulp

one?"

School was worse than before.

It looked like I.Q., Priscilla, and I were about the only ones who hadn't fallen under the worms' power . . . because we were the only ones who hadn't eaten any.

But that didn't stop the other kids from trying to make us.

"Just one," they kept begging. "Just take one bite. That's all."

But we would not give in.

"Look what you're doing!" I shouted. "Look how the worms are controlling you!"

But nobody would listen. Not even our teacher, Mrs. Hooplesnort.

In fact, worms became part of every subject she taught.

For starters, there was . . .

HISTORY

"As we know," she said, "Christopher Columbus sailed across the ocean in 1492 and discovered . . . worms."

(See what I mean?)

Then there was . . .

GEOGRAPHY

"The president lives at the *Worm* House in *Worm*ington, D.C. . . ."

And let's not forget . . .

MATH

"As you can see, if we have 7 worms and add 9 worms, we get 8 worms."

"Uh, Mrs. Hooplesnort?" I raised my hand. "Isn't the right answer 16 worms?"

She frowned. "Why would there be 16 worms when they're so tasty?"

With that, she took half of them and shoved them into her . . .

chomp, chomp
gulp, gulp
BURP!

mouth.

Then, remembering her manners, she turned to me and asked, "Would you like the others?"

If I had shaken my head any harder it would have fallen off.

Last, but not least, there was my favorite subject . . .

LUNCH

The cafeteria was crawling with worms. They were everywhere. On the floor, on the tables, in the sandwiches!

And everybody loved them!

Everybody but I.Q., Priscilla, and me. Oh, there was one other . . .

Splat, the Wonder-dud, er, dog! He was crawling out of my backpack.

"Splat!" I cried. "What are you doing here?"

He leaped from my backpack and hit the ground with a huge

K-SPLAT

(Like I said, he's not so graceful.)

He looked at me, took a deep breath, then in his bravest, most heroic voice . . . he whimpered like a baby.

(Okay, so he's not exactly brave, either.)

"Perhaps he was too *(sniff)* frightened to remain at home," I.Q. said. "Perhaps—"

Suddenly, he was interrupted by a dozen kids. They started toward us and began chanting:

"Eat worms! Eat worms! Eat worms!"

They stretched out their hands. In them they held hundreds of the creepy-crawlies.

"Eat worms! Eat worms! Eat worms!"

"Uh, Bernie?"

"Yeah, I.Q.?"

"I believe *(sniff)* they wish us to digest some worms."

"We're not interested," Priscilla said.

"Eat worms! Eat worms! Eat worms!"

"It doesn't appear *(sniff, sniff)* that they are giving us a choice."

They closed in around us.

Splat growled. He'd seen all those doggie hero TV shows. He knew it was time to save the day. He knew it was time to be a hero. He knew it was time to leap into my arms and shake with fear.

Unfortunately, his leaper was a little lopsided.

Instead of landing in my arms, he hit one of the straps of my backpack—actually, a little electronic button on one of the straps. Suddenly,

whop-whop-whop-whop

a propeller sprang from the backpack.

It started lifting us off the ground.

"Bernie, what are you doing?" Priscilla cried.

"I don't know! It's my secret agent backpack!"

The kids kept closing in:

"Eat worms! Eat worms! Eat worms!"

"Bernie! Get down here and help us!" she shouted.

I nodded and hit another button on the strap. Nothing happened, except—

"WHOA!"

Now we were flying upside down!

"Eat worms! Eat worms! Eat worms!"

"BERNIE!"

I hit another button. We started flying sideways, back and forth across the room.

"WHOA...

WAAA...

WEEE..."

"Eat worms! Eat worms! Eat worms!"

I hit another button and we flipped right side up again.

Well, *I* was right side up.

So was Splat. Except he was *on top* of the propeller blades. Now the poor pup was going around and around . . . and around some more.

"Eat worms! Eat worms! Eat worms!"

"BERNIE!"

They'd nearly reached my friends.

It was time to do something crazy.

It was time to do something Dad would never do. . . .

It was time to read the instructions!

I found a paper in my backpack and pulled it out.

It read:

TO STOP
PRESS THE STOP BUTTON

What a great idea!

I pressed the button labeled STOP.

The propeller folded up into my pack and we fell back into the crowd.

This was good and bad.

Good, if you wanted to hang out with your friends.

Bad, if you hated the taste of worms!

CHAPTER 4

A Time for Action

"Eat worms! Eat worms! Eat worms!"

They were all around us and closing in.

"What do we do?" Priscilla shouted.

"I don't know!"

"Eat worms! Eat worms! Eat worms!"

"What about your secret agent watch?" I.Q. yelled. "The one with all the buttons?"

I looked down at my wrist watch. He was right. There were a trillion buttons to push. But which one?

"Eat worms! Eat worms! Eat—"

Using my genius brain, I did what any genius would do: I closed my eyes and pushed any ol' button.

Suddenly, a green beam shot out of my watch.

I pointed it at the crowd and . . .

"Eeeeeeeeaaaaaattttttt woooooooorrrrrrrrrmmmmmmssssss. . . ."

"What's going on?" Priscilla cried.

"The beam is placing everyone in slow motion!" I.Q. shouted.

He was right. Everyone was moving a lot slower.

"Eeeeeeeeaaaaaattttttt woooooooorrrrrrrrrmmmmmmssssss. . . ."

"Come on!" Priscilla yelled. "Let's get out of here!"

It was so crowded that we had to duck under arms and crawl between legs.

Unfortunately, this called for coordination. Something I.Q. has none of. I don't want to say he's clumsy, but he's the only kid I know who has to wear a bike helmet just to walk up stairs. "Help me!" he shouted.

I looked down at him. He was stuck between some of the legs.

"I'm caught," he said. He looked up to me. "I can't—"

And that's when it happened. . . .

That's when a worm fell from some kid's hand. It dropped straight into I.Q.'s mouth.

First, I.Q. kind of . . .

chok-ed, *chok*-ed

then he kind of . . .

gasp-ed, *gasp*-ed

and finally he . . .

swallow-ed, *swallow*-ed.

"I.Q.!" I cried. "Are you all right?"

"Mmm." He licked his lips. "These are rather tasty."

Before I could stop him, he grabbed some more from the kid's hand.

"I.Q.!"

He shoved them into his mouth.

"Excellent!" He grinned. "You two *must* try these!"

"I.Q.!" Priscilla started toward him but I caught her.

"It's no good," I said. "He's eaten one."

"But . . ."

"We can't help him now. Come on!"

I felt bad leaving I.Q. behind. But like I told Big Guy, a fellow's got to look out for himself.

We raced into the hall.

Another crowd of kids was coming from the other direction.

"Eeeeeeeeaaaaaattttttt
wooooooooorrrrrrrrmmmmmmsssss. . . ."

"There are too many to go through!"
Priscilla cried.

I looked around and spotted a door
beside us.

"In here!" I shouted.

Priscilla gave me one of her 'you gotta
be kidding' looks.

"What?" I yelled.

She pointed to the sign. It read:

BOYS
REST ROOM

"You got a better idea?" I asked.

She looked up the hall in front of us.

"Eeeeeeeeaaaaaattttttt
wooooooooorrrrrrrrmmmmmmsssss. . . ."

She looked down the hall behind us.

"Eeeeeeeeaaaaaattttttt
wooooooooorrrrrrrrrmmmmmmsssss. . . ."

There was no way out.

"All right," she sighed. "But if we die,
you're going to live to regret it!"

I grabbed her hand and we ran inside.

We'd barely stepped into the room
before . . .

"Agent Dingledorf . . . Secret Agent
Dingledorf?"

I looked at Priscilla.

She looked at me.

"Agent Dingledorf?"

I swallowed. "Who . . . who said that?"

"It's . . . me, Big Guy."

"Where . . . where are you?"

"Here," the voice called. "Over here!"

We turned to one of the stalls. The door was wide open and nobody was inside.

"Agent Dingledorf . . ."

We inched our way forward.

"Hurry," the voice said, "we haven't much time."

At last we were inside the stall. But there was still nobody—

"Down here!"

We leaned over and looked into the toilet bowl. Sure enough, Big Guy was inside waving! "Hi, there."

But he was only an inch tall. And he was standing on the deck of a tiny boat.

"What are you doing?!" I shouted.

"I've come to save you!" he called. "And to convince you to save the world!"

"I told you, I'm not interested," I said.

"But what about I.Q.?" Big Guy called. "What about all the others?"

"I'm sorry, they'll just have to—"

The bathroom door creaked open. The crowd came into view. They continued moving toward us in slow motion.

"Eeeeeeeeaaaaaatttttt wooooooooorrrrrrrrmmmmmmssssss. . . ."

"We're trapped!" Priscilla cried. "What do we do?"

"Eeeeeeeeaaaaaatttttt wooooooooorrrrrrrrmmmmmmssssss. . . ."

"Hurry!" Big Guy shouted. "Jump in here and join me!"

"We're too big!" I cried. "We won't fit!"

"I've got the Gizmo Gun!" he yelled. He pulled out something that looked like a green-and-yellow squirt gun. "It will make you smaller!"

The crowd closed in.

"Eeeeeeeeaaaaaattttt woooooooorrrrrrrrmmmmmmsssss. . . ."

"Hurry!" Big Guy shouted. "Hold hands and jump!"

"But—"

"Eeeeeeeeaaaaaattttt . . ."

"Jump!"

" . . . woooooooorrrrrrrrmmmmmmsssss. . . ."

I reached out and grabbed Priscilla's hand. "Here goes nothing!" I yelled.

"When you're right, you're right," she shouted.

We took a deep breath and jumped . . .

"AUGHHHH!"

Big Guy fired the Gizmo Gun. Purple light with pink polka dots struck us, and our cry shrank to . . .

"aughhhh"

as our tiny bodies tumbled onto the deck of his tiny boat.

I jumped up and looked around.

We'd both shrunk to the size of Big Guy. It was pretty cool.

Well, except for . . .

"WOOF!"

I looked up and saw a giant monster dog staring down on us.

"Splat!" Priscilla cried. "We forgot Splat!"

She was right. High above us, Splat was barking and jumping in excitement.

"WOOF! WOOF!"

"Take it easy, boy!" I shouted. "You're giving me a headache."

He dropped his nose just inches from us.

"WOOF! WOOF! WOOF!"

The good news was, Splat does not drink water from the toilet bowl. (Or eat tiny people on tiny boats.)

The bad news was, he kept jumping up and down and barking until . . . his front paw accidentally hit the toilet handle and . . .

K-FLUSH

water poured in from all sides.

"What's happening?" I yelled.

"Hang on!" Big Guy shouted. "Looks like we're taking a little sewer tour!"

CHAPTER 5

Down the Drain . . .

I suppose being an inch tall and riding through sewers can be great fun. Especially if you like . . .

- drowning in a gazillion gallons of water,

- spinning and tumbling like you're in a blender gone crazy, and

- meeting rats the size of Ford pickups.

(Don't get me wrong. I've got nothing against rats. They make swell pets. But when you're *teeny tiny,* they can be, oh, I don't know . . . *TERRIBLY TERRIFYING!)*

One of the furry fellows spotted our boat. He swam toward us and started

SQUEAK-SQUEAK-ing.

"What's he saying?" I cried over the roaring water and waves.

"It's been a long time since I spoke rat-ese," Big Guy shouted.

SQUEAK-SQUEAK

"You must have some idea," Priscilla yelled.

Big Guy nodded. "He either wants to have us over for dinner tonight or he wants to have us . . .

SQUEAK-SQUEAK

for dinner."

Suddenly, the giant fur ball opened his mouth and snapped at us.

We all screamed and leaped back.

"He thinks we're a rat snack!" I cried.

Another wave hit the boat. We cried and hung on for our lives. But our furry foe just rode the wave like some surfer dude.

"What do we do?" Priscilla yelled.

"Dingledorf!" Big Guy shouted. "Use your Transformer Beam."

"My what?"

"On your belt buckle!"

As usual, I had no idea what he was talking about. But I looked down and noticed that a tiny keyboard had appeared on my belt buckle.

"Type in the word 'CAT'!" he shouted.

"What?"

"The beam will make us look like cats. It will scare him away!"

"That's a great idea!" Priscilla yelled.
I reached down and typed the word

$$CAT$$

Well, at least that's what *I* typed.

Unfortunately, the damp keyboard was shorting out from all that water. So instead of coming out "C A T," it sparked, sputtered, and came out

$$CHEESE$$

Suddenly, we looked like three pieces of cheese!

If Fur Ball was hungry before, he was downright starved now.

"What do we do?!" I cried.

"Know any good prayers?" Priscilla shouted.

Just then the rat leaped toward us. Big Guy steered the boat into another wave.

It was the biggest yet. Suddenly, we were up to our waists in water. We clung to the rail for our lives.

"Hang on!" he shouted.

"Where are we going?" I cried.

He yelled, "I'll tell you when we get there!"

After a bunch more . . .

splashing,

        screaming,

                and drowning,

we popped up out of a floor drain at the local shopping mall.

"Cool!" Priscilla said as we crawled up onto the floor tile.

She was right. It was nice to breathe something other than water.

But it was *not so nice* still being one inch tall.

And it was worse than *not so nice* almost getting stepped on by a million shoppers.

"Now what?" I shouted.

"Hold still!" Big Guy yelled as he pointed his Gizmo Gun.

He zapped us with more purple and pink polka-dot lights.

Immediately, all three of us became our normal size.

But nobody noticed. The shoppers were too busy shoving worms into their mouths.

That's right, there was more worm action here than at my school.

Only, they weren't just *eating* worms. They were also buying and selling them.

Up ahead was a "J.C. Wormies" store . . . where people were trying on clothes made of the slimy slipperies.

Next to that was a waterbed store. But instead of water, the beds were full of . . . (don't even make me say it).

Then, of course, there were the fast-food restaurants . . . "Kentucky Fried Worms," "Worm in the Box," and the always popular "McWormald's."

Suddenly, my shoes began to speak:

"Hurl Alert!
Hurl Alert!"

I looked down at my feet. My shoes were flashing red, blue, and green lights!

"What's that?" I shouted to Big Guy.

"It's your B.A.D.D. alarm!" he yelled.

"My what??"

"It goes off whenever you're close to a B.A.D.D. agent. Or when you listen to too much country-western music!"

"Hurl Alert!
Hurl Alert!"

He pointed to the balcony. "Up there! I see one!"

"Where?" I yelled.

"There, at the pet shop!"

I barely had time to look before I heard:

"Eat worms! Eat worms! Eat worms!"

The shoppers had finally noticed that we weren't chomping away on the creepy-crawlies (or wearing them). They had started toward us.

"Eat worms! Eat worms! Eat worms!"

"You two go ahead!" Big Guy shouted. "I'll hold them off."

They closed in.

"Eat worms! Eat worms! Eat worms!"

"What's going to happen to you?" I yelled.

"Don't worry about me! Just get that B.A.D.D. agent!"

I shook my head. "You need to look out for yourself!"

"No!" he yelled. "This is exactly what I've been telling you. Sometimes you've got to look out for others first."

"But—"

"Go!"

Before I could argue, he turned and started toward the shoppers.

"Eat worms! Eat worms! Eat worms!"

"We've got to help him!" Priscilla shouted.

But it was too late. They'd already surrounded him.

"Come on!" I cried. "We've got to get out of here!"

"But—"

"Come on!"

I grabbed her hand and we started to run.

"Are we going to the pet shop?" she shouted.

A good question . . .

Did I want to catch the B.A.D.D. agent and save the world?

Or did I want to run away and save my skin?

"Eat worms! Eat worms! Eat worms!"

I didn't know. The only thing I did know was that I'd have to make a decision . . . and I'd have to make it fast!

CHAPTER 6

Showdown

"**S**ecret Agent Dingledorf!"

The voice wasn't Big Guy! It was coming from the pet shop.

"Secret Agent Dingledorf!"

As we all know, I'm Bernie Dingledorf, not Secret Agent Dingledorf.

"Secret Agent Dingledorf!"

But as we also know, I'm the only one who seems to remember that little fact.

I looked up and there was the B.A.D.D. agent.

He stood at the entrance of the shop.

He was not smiling. He was not waving. He wasn't even offering free samples of Worm Chow.

Instead, he was typing something on the keyboard of his belt buckle. A belt buckle that looked exactly like mine. (I guess all secret agents shop at the same secret agent store.)

Suddenly, before my eyes, he turned into a giant bat. I knew he was still an agent. It was just a disguise.

But when he spread out his wings and started flying toward us, Priscilla and I decided it would be a good time to scream and run for our lives!

As we ran, I reached down to my secret agent belt buckle. I also typed the word "B A T."

Unfortunately, the ol' keyboard was still shorting out. So instead of "B A T," it came out:

HAT

No problem. Except I suddenly had no legs, a giant bill, and the name *Los Angeles Dodgers* written across my front.

Again, no problem, except I'm a Yankees fan. Oh, and since I didn't have any legs, it was a little hard running.

I looked up. The bat was chasing Priscilla toward the pet shop.

I tried to warn her. I opened my mouth and shouted, "   !" (Which is exactly the sound baseball caps make when they try to shout.)

I reached down to my belt buckle and tried again. This time it didn't short out. Yea! This time it *really did* type "B A T."

But instead of sprouting wings and flying, I became long and skinny and round.

The good news was, *Los Angeles Dodgers* disappeared from my front.

The bad news was, it was replaced by *Louisville Slugger*.

I turned myself into a bat, all right. A baseball bat!!

"Help me, Bernie!"

I looked up. The B.A.D.D. agent had changed back. Now he was dragging Priscilla into the pet shop.

"Help me!" she cried.

I thought of what Big Guy had said about looking out for others.

"Help me!"

I thought of how terrible I felt when we left I.Q. behind.

"Help me!"

I thought of how I wanted to save my neck . . . but knew I should save Priscilla's instead.

I turned off my belt buckle and became a kid again.

Then I raced to the pet shop.

"Let her go!" I shouted.

But B.A.D.D. Boy pulled her closer and laughed:

"Moo-hoo-haa-haa-haa . . ."

I don't want to be rude, but on the Creep-You-Out Scale of 1 to 10, I'd give that laugh an 11.

"And so we meet again, Secret Agent Dingledorf!"

"I'm not a secret agent!" I cried.

"Right, and I'm not Boris the B.A.D.D. Boy."

"You're not?"

"Not what?"

"Boris the whatever . . ."

"Of course I am."

"You just said you weren't."

"Weren't what?"

"Boris."

"I was making a point."

"I thought you were giving me a name."

He rubbed his temples. "You're giving me a headache. Can we just get on with the showdown?"

"The what?"

"The part where we fight until the finish." (Or until one of us runs home to mommy.)

Before I could answer, he started typing on his belt buckle again.

Poor guy. All he had was the belt buckle. His agency didn't give him nearly as many gizmos to play with as mine did. Maybe for Christmas I could get him a nice helicopter backpack . . . or jet-powered dental floss . . . or—

Suddenly, he turned himself into a

giant wizard . . . complete with wand and dunce cap. (He'd obviously been reading too many Hairy Potty books.)

I reached to my belt buckle and also typed "W I Z A R D."

Well, almost. The keyboard was nearly dry and only missed it by one letter. But there's a world of difference between "W I Z A R D" and

L I Z A R D

Talk about gross. Talk about embarrassing. Talk about wondering if I had to start eating flies.

Bzzzzzzzzz

Uh-oh, there's one now.

But this was no time for a snack. Our

battle with Boris the B.A.D.D. Boy had barely begun.

He reached to his buckle and typed:

$$DOG$$

Immediately, he was on all fours and chasing me around the shop.

"Bark! Bark! Bark!"

Obviously, the fellow was hungry for a little lizard treat.

A little lizard treat that just happened to be me!

CHAPTER 7

Dog Fight

So, there I was . . . looking like a lizard and jogging around the pet shop. (Do lizards jog?)

B.A.D.D. Boy kept barking at my heels. (Do lizards have heels?)

All the birds in the shop were *chirping,* all the dogs were *barking,* and all the fish were, uh, *glugging.*

We ran back and forth and back and forth. When we got tired of that, we ran forth and back and forth and back.

Yes sir, it was great fun . . . except for the part of nearly getting eaten a few thousand times.

Finally, I'd had enough. If he wanted a dog fight, I'd give him a dog fight. I reached down to my belt buckle and typed "D O G." But the keyboard still hadn't dried out. So instead of a dog, I became a:

HOG

Which explains why I started oinking and looking for a mud hole.

Unfortunately, this didn't stop the B.A.D.D. boy bow-wow. Instead of lizard meat, he suddenly had an urge for . . . porkchops!

I typed again. But instead of "D O G," it came out:

LOG

Again, it was close. But not close enough.

Now B.A.D.D. Boy wanted to play fetch. With me as the stick!

I decided to try something completely different. Instead of "D O G," I typed "P U P P Y."

The keyboard only missed it by a couple of letters.

Instead of becoming a "P U P P Y," I became:

POOPY

Things were definitely starting to stink . . . (in more ways than one).

The shoppers began entering the store. They headed straight toward me, chanting, "Eat worms! Eat worms! Eat worms!"

It looked like my goose was cooked.

honk-honk

(Oops, didn't know there were geese in the pet shop. Sorry, fellows.)

. . . It looked like my fish was fried.

glug-glug

(Oh, yeah, there were all those fish, too. Sorry, guys.)

Luckily, before I could hurt anyone else's feelings . . .

"WOOF! WOOF!"

I looked up. There was Splat the Wonder-dog, coming to my rescue!

"Attaboy, Splat!" I shouted as I turned off the belt buckle and became a kid again. "Come on!"

He raced toward me. He was going to save the world. He was going to be a hero.

He was going to—

"No, Splat! That's a window! You're running straight into a—"

K-Splat

So much for being a hero.

But Splat wasn't going to let a little thing like being knocked out stop him.

No sir. He still remembered those TV shows. He still knew what Wonder-dogs did. (He also knew his name was on the cover of these books.)

So he leaped back to his feet and ran into the shop. And, with the greatest speed . . . he found an open dog-food bag and started to eat. (He likes eating.)

"No, Splat!" I shouted. "I need your help over here!"

He turned to me, licked his lips, and

BURP-ed.

(He likes eating a lot.)
Suddenly,

"Moo-hoo-haa-haa-haa . . ."

there was that creepy laugh again.

I spun around to see B.A.D.D. Boy right behind me.

He was holding Priscilla. She already had a handful of worms in her mouth.

Oh, no!

He started toward me.

Double *oh, no!*

"Your time is up, Dingledorf!" He sneered. "You're the only one not under my power!"

He continued toward me. . . .

Three steps to go.

(What will I do?)

Two steps to go.

(I'm not kidding. Anybody got a suggestion?)

One step to go.

(Any suggestion will do.)

"WOOF! WOOF!"

All right, Splat! He decided to rescue me, after all. He—

Burp, Burp
BELCH

finished off the dog food and was looking for more.

In his search he leaped up to a table. Then he leaped to the top row of shelves. At least that's what he tried to do. But we already know his leaper is a little lame.

"No, Splat! Look out for the fishtanks! You're going to knock down the—"

K-rash! K-bang!
tinkle, tinkle, tinkle!

The entire shelf of fishtanks came down.

No problem. Except they came down onto another shelf of tanks below them,

K-rash! K-bang!
tinkle, tinkle, tinkle!

which came down onto the shelf below them, which . . . well, you get the picture.

Soon, a million fishtanks had shattered all over the floor.

And from each of those million fishtanks came about a hundred million little

glug-glug-glug

fish flapping around.

Yes sir, things were looking worse by the second.

Or were they?

CHAPTER 8

The Case Closes

When we left Splat the Wonder-dog, he was busy saving the world from worms.

But how do you save the world by knocking over a gazillion fishtanks?

Glad you asked.

What lives in fishtanks?

Okay, that one was pretty easy. Here's another . . .

What do fish eat?

I'm thinking of a word starting with the letter *W* and ending in "O-R-M-S."

Very good.

Quicker than you can say "biological food chain" (or figure out what it means), the fish began eating up the worms.

They ate worms

GULP GULP GULP

on the floor.
    They leaped up and ate worms

GULP GULP GULP

in the hands of the shoppers.
    They even jumped off the balcony and ate worms

GULP GULP GULP

on the lower level.
    "Way to go, Splat!" I shouted. "Way to go!"
    "Stop!" B.A.D.D. Boy shouted. "What do you think you're doing?"
    "We're freeing all these people from your worm power!" I yelled.

"No fair!" he cried. "Why don't you mind your own business?!"

"Because that's been my problem!"

"What?"

"I've been minding my own business. I've been thinking only of myself."

"So?"

"So these people *are* my business. We're all each other's business."

"Oh, no," B.A.D.D. Boy groaned. "It sounds like you're getting ready to give one of those good-guy speeches."

"Hey, that's a great idea!" I said.

I raced to the railing and looked down at the shoppers. Without the worms, their minds were already starting to clear.

"Friends!" I shouted. "Friends!"

They looked up at me.

"You've all been under the spell of these worms."

They kept listening.

"We broke their power over you, but you must not eat any more."

They began to nod. "But we must not stop here," I shouted. "We must go out and help our friends and neighbors. We must take these fish into our city to eat all the worms! We must save everyone from worm power!"

The people began to clap.

I spotted Big Guy. He gave me a thumbs-up, and I continued. "Because that is our responsibility!" I shouted. "We must look out for each other. We must be there to help the other guy!"

The people cheered. They gathered the fish into their arms. They dumped them into shopping bags. They even piled them into their baby strollers.

Then they headed out into the streets.

Soon the entire city would be saved.
After that, the world.

"*Woof! Woof!*"

I turned to Splat.
His little tail wagged with excitement.
His roly-poly body shook with joy.
His mouth . . .

chomp, chomp, chomp-ed

with delight as he found another open
bag of dog food.
And B.A.D.D. Boy?
I looked around the pet shop.
He was nowhere to be found.
But somehow, I knew I'd see him
again. I knew this wasn't the last time
we'd meet.

And so, we headed for home.

Home, where Mom had fixed a nice spaghetti dinner (that didn't wiggle or squirm). Home, where my three sisters just kept talking. . . .

"I could have just died when Jeremy smiled at Heather instead of me. . . ."

and talking . . .

"Charlie told Chelsea not to tell Chad what Cheri told . . .

and talking some more . . .

"These earrings are sooo cool, and they only cost . . ."

Yes sir, everything had returned to normal. Everything was just like it used to be before—

beep-beep-beep-beep

"Dear?" Mom asked. "Is that your underwear ringing again?"

Anyway, like I was saying . . . Everything had returned to normal. Everything was just like it used to be before—

beep-beep-beep-beep

"Sweetheart," Mom asked, "aren't you going to answer it?"

I gave a sigh. I didn't want to admit it. But it looked like ringing underwear had become part of my new and *not-so-*normal life.

A life dedicated to helping people.

A life dedicated to thinking of others.
A life as Secret Agent

beep-beep-beep-beep

Dingledorf . . . and his trusty dog, . . .

"Woof! Woof!"

Splat.